# Goodnight Racism

Ibram X. Kendi ★ illustrated by Cbabi Bayoc

Kokila

*To Imani and the awesome power of*
*our children to dream and create anew.*
*—I. X. K.*

*I dedicate this to my three dreamers: Jurni, Ajani, and Birago.*
*—C. B.*

KOKILA
An imprint of Penguin Random House LLC, New York

First published in the United States of America by Kokila, an imprint of Penguin Random House LLC, 2022

Text copyright © 2022 by Ibram X. Kendi
Illustrations copyright © 2022 by Cbabi Bayoc

Kokila & colophon are registered trademarks of Penguin Random House LLC.

Visit us online at penguinrandomhouse.com.

Library of Congress Cataloging-in-Publication Data is available.

Printed in the United States of America

ISBN 9780593110515
10 9 8 7 6 5 4 3 2 1
PC

Design by Jasmin Rubero
Text set in Cream

*The art for the book was created digitally, rendered with textured brushes in Procreate.*

Outside the window,
peeking down from the night sky,
the moon watches over us.

She sees kids
smiling at dinner tables

and yawning in their beds.

But some kids
do not have food,
do not have beds
because of unfair rules
and unjust treatment.

The moon sees all kids—
whoever they are,
wherever they are—
and shines her light on them.

The moon wants her light
to kiss *every* child goodnight.
The moon delights
when every child falls asleep.

Because the moon knows when we sleep,
we dream.

When we dream,
we imagine what is possible,
what the world can be,
and the moon glows a little brighter, whispering,

*Dream, my child; imagine, my child.*
*A new world—a new future—awaits.*

A world where all people are safe,
no matter how they look,

FRESH BAKED
**PEACE**

**FAIRNESS**

TRUE

**ACCEPTANCE**

**EQUALITY**

**FUN**

Fresh Squeezed

**COMPASSION**

LEMON
SHAKE-UPS

HEART
VIBES

OZEN
NANAS

FRIES

POSITIVE

Proud
DAD
365

how they worship,

or how they love.

A world where all kids have the same chance
to have peace,
to have joy,
to have a childhood.

A world where all people breathe fresh air
and have what they need
to feed their minds and bodies.

A world where our rules open doors,
open minds,
and create equity
and justice for all.

*Dream, my child; create, my child.*
*A new world—a new future—awaits.*

Goodnight unfair rules.
Goodnight cruelty.

Goodnight injustice.
Goodnight inequality.

Goodnight hate.
Goodnight hurt.

Goodnight racism.
Goodnight.